GOOD
WORK,
AMELIA
BEDELIA

GOOD WORK, AMELIA BEDELIA

by Peggy Parish

pictures by Lynn Sweat

AN AVON CAMELOT BOOK

3rd grade reading level has been determined by using the Fry Readability Scale.

AVON BOOKS
A division of
The Hearst Corporation
1350 Avenue of the Americas
New York, New York 10019

Copyright © 1976 by Margaret Parish
Illustrations copyright © 1976 by Lynn Sweat
Published by arrangement with William Morrow and Company, Inc.
Library of Congress Catalog Card Number: 75-20360
ISBN: 0-380-49171-0

First Avon Camelot Printing: March 1980

CAMELOT TRADEMARK REG. U.S. PAT. OFF. AND IN OTHER COUNTRIES, MARCA REGISTRADA, HECHO EN U.S.A.

Printed in the U.S.A.

BAN   36   35   34   33   32   31   30   29

For Sam and David Rogers
with love

"Amelia Bedelia," called Mr. Rogers.

"Is the coffee ready?"

"Coming right up," said Amelia Bedelia.

She poured a cup of coffee.

She took it into the dining room.

"There," said Amelia Bedelia.

"Would you like something more?"

"Yes," said Mr. Rogers.

"Toast and an egg."

"Fine," said Amelia Bedelia.

She went into the kitchen.

Very quickly

Amelia Bedelia was back.

Mr. Rogers picked up the egg.

He broke it over his toast.

"Confound it, Amelia Bedelia!"

he said. "I didn't say raw egg!"

"But you didn't say to cook it,"
said Amelia Bedelia.

Mr. Rogers threw down his napkin.
"Oh, go fly a kite," he said.

Amelia Bedelia looked surprised.

"All right," she said. "If you say so."

Soon Amelia Bedelia was out in a field.

She had a kite.

"Now that was nice of Mr. Rogers,"

she said. "I do love to fly kites.

But I better get back.

Mrs. Rogers might need me."

Sure enough, Mrs. Rogers was calling,
"Amelia Bedelia."

"Here I am," said Amelia Bedelia.

"There's a lot to do,"
  said Mrs. Rogers.

"Do you know how to make bread?"

"I make good corn bread,"
  said Amelia Bedelia.

"No, I want white bread,"
  said Mrs. Rogers.

"You are a good cook.
  Just do what the recipe says."

"All right," said Amelia Bedelia.

"Here's a list of the other things
    I want you to do,"
    said Mrs. Rogers.
"I'll be out until dinner time."
"Don't worry," said Amelia Bedelia.
"I'll get everything done."
    Mrs. Rogers left.

"I'll start with that bread,"
said Amelia Bedelia.
She read the recipe.
"Do tell," she said.
"I never knew
bread did magic things."

Amelia Bedelia got everything
she needed.
Quickly she mixed the dough.

Amelia Bedelia

set the pan on the table.

"Now," she said,

"you're supposed to rise.

This I've got to see."

Amelia Bedelia sat down to watch.

But nothing happened.

"Maybe you don't like to be watched.

I'll come back," said Amelia Bedelia.

"Let's see."

Amelia Bedelia got her list.

"Clean out the ashes

in the parlor fireplace.

Fill the wood box."

Amelia Bedelia went into the parlor.

She cleaned out the ashes.

And Amelia Bedelia filled

the wood box.

"That's done," said Amelia Bedelia.

"What's next?"

She read, "Pot the window box plants.

Put the pots in the parlor."

Amelia Bedelia went outside.

She counted the plants.

Then she went into the kitchen.

"My goodness," she said.

"I need every pot for this."

So she took them all.

Amelia Bedelia potted those plants.

And she took them inside.

"Now I better tend to that bread,"
said Amelia Bedelia.

She went into the kitchen.

But the bread still sat on the table.

"Now look here," she said.

"You are supposed to rise.
Then I'm supposed to punch you down.
How can I punch if you don't rise?"

Amelia Bedelia sat down to think.

"Maybe that pan is too heavy,"
she said.

"I better help it rise."

Amelia Bedelia got some string.

She worked for a bit.

And that bread began to rise.

"That should be high enough,"
said Amelia Bedelia.

"I'll just let you stay there awhile."

Amelia Bedelia picked up her list.

"'Make a sponge cake.'"

Amelia Bedelia read that again.

"I know about a lot of cakes,"
she said.

"And I never heard tell of that.
But if she wants a sponge cake,
I'll make her a sponge cake."

Amelia Bedelia put a little of this
and some of that into a bowl.
She mixed and mixed.
"Now for the sponge," she said.
Amelia Bedelia got a sponge.
She snipped it into small pieces.
"There," she said.
"Into the cake you go."

Soon the sponge cake was baking.

"I don't think Mr. Rogers

will like this cake,"

said Amelia Bedelia.

"I'll make my kind of cake too.

He does love butterscotch icing."

So Amelia Bedelia

baked another cake.

"There now," she said.

"I'll surprise him."

Amelia Bedelia put

the butterscotch cake in the cupboard.

She put the sponge cake on a shelf.

"My, this is a busy day,"
said Amelia Bedelia. ·
"Let's see what's next.
'Call Alcolu. Ask him to patch
the front door screen.'"
Amelia Bedelia shook her head.
"Alcolu can't patch anything,"
she said. "I better do that myself."
She got what she needed.

And Amelia Bedelia patched that screen.

Amelia Bedelia looked at the time.

"Oh," she said.

"I better get dinner started.

Let me see what she wants."

She read the list.

"'A chicken dinner will be fine.'"

Amelia Bedelia shook her head.

"What will she think of next?" she said.

"Well, that won't take long to fix."

Amelia Bedelia got everything ready.

She set the table.

Then she sat down to rest.

Soon Mr. and Mrs. Rogers came home.

"Amelia Bedelia," yelled Mr. Rogers.

"Coming," called Amelia Bedelia.

"What is that awful cloth
   on the front door?" said Mrs. Rogers.

"You said to patch the screen,"
said Amelia Bedelia.
"Can't patch without a patch."

They went into the parlor.

"All my good pots!" said Mrs. Rogers.

"And bad ones too,"
said Amelia Bedelia.

Mr. Rogers looked at the wood box.

He shook his head.

But he didn't say a word.

They went into the kitchen.

"The sponge cake is pretty,"
said Mrs. Rogers.

"At least that's done right."

Something caught Mr. Rogers's eye.

He looked up.

"What in tarnation is that?" he said.

"The bread!" said Amelia Bedelia.

"I plumb forgot it.

Do let me punch it down quick."

She climbed up on a chair.

Amelia Bedelia began to punch.

Mr. and Mrs. Rogers just stared.

The bread plopped to the floor.

"Did I see what I thought I saw?"

said Mr. Rogers.

"You did," said Mrs. Rogers.

"Now," said Amelia Bedelia,

"dinner is ready when you are."

"Well, you can cook," said Mrs. Rogers.

"Dinner should be good."

"I hope so," said Mr. Rogers.

"I'm hungry."

"Just serve the plates,"

said Mrs. Rogers.

Mr. and Mrs. Rogers sat at the table.
Amelia Bedelia brought in the plates.

Mr. and Mrs. Rogers stared at the plates.

"But, but, that's cracked corn.

It's all kinds of awful things,"

said Mrs. Rogers.

"You said chicken dinner,"

said Amelia Bedelia.

"That's what chickens eat for dinner."

Mrs. Rogers was too angry to speak.

"Take this mess away,"

said Mr. Rogers.

Mrs. Rogers said,
"Serve the cake and coffee."
Amelia Bedelia did.

Mr. Rogers took a big bite of cake.

He spluttered and spit it out.

"What in tarnation is in that?" he said.

"Sponge," said Amelia Bedelia.

"Mrs. Rogers said

to make a sponge cake."

Suddenly Mr. Rogers laughed.

He roared.

Mrs. Rogers looked at the lumpy cake.

Then she laughed too.

"But I'm still hungry,"
said Mr. Rogers.

"I can fix that," said Amelia Bedelia.

"I have a surprise for you."

"Oh, no!" said Mr. Rogers.

"I can't stand another one,"
said Mrs. Rogers.

Amelia Bedelia brought in milk
and her butterscotch cake.
"Ahh," said Mr. Rogers.
"Hurry," said Mrs. Rogers.
"Give me some."
Soon the whole cake was gone.

"How do you do it, Amelia Bedelia?"
said Mr. Rogers. "One minute
we're hopping mad at you."
"And the next, we know we can't
do without you," said Mrs. Rogers.

Amelia Bedelia smiled.

"I guess I just understand your ways,"
she said.

Join all the fun and surprises with

The Birthday Girls

by Jean Thesman

MIRROR, MIRROR
Ceegee's Story

76271-4/$2.99 US/$3.50 Can

Ceegee knew that having a birthday party that brought together all the kids born on the same day at the same hospital would be different—good and bad. The good part is she makes two great new friends. The terrible part is that they share their birthday with one person who manages to ruin everyone's day.

Don't Miss These Other
Birthday Girl Reunion Party Stories

I'M NOT TELLING
Jill's Story

76523-3/$2.99 US/$3.50 Can

WHO AM I, ANYWAY?
Nancy's Story

76524-1/$2.99 US/$3.50 Can

Celebrating 40 Years of Cleary Kids!

CAMELOT presents
BEVERLY CLEARY FAVORITES!

☐ **HENRY HUGGINS**
70912-0 ($3.99 US/$4.99 Can)

☐ **HENRY AND BEEZUS**
70914-7 ($3.99 US/$4.99 Can)

☐ **HENRY AND THE
CLUBHOUSE**
70915-5 ($3.99 US/$4.99 Can)

☐ **ELLEN TEBBITS**
70913-9 ($3.99 US/$4.99 Can)

☐ **HENRY AND RIBSY**
70917-1 ($3.99 US/$4.99 Can)

☐ **BEEZUS AND RAMONA**
70918-X ($3.99 US/$4.99 Can)

☐ **RAMONA AND HER FATHER**
70916-3 ($3.99 US/$4.99 Can)

☐ **MITCH AND AMY**
70925-2 ($3.99 US/$4.99 Can)

☐ **RUNAWAY RALPH**
70953-8 ($3.99 US/$4.99 Can)

☐ **RAMONA QUIMBY, AGE 8**
70956-2 ($3.99 US/$4.99 Can)

☐ **RIBSY**
70955-4 ($3.99 US/$4.99 Can)

☐ **STRIDER**
71236-9 ($3.99 US/$4.99 Can)

☐ **HENRY AND THE
PAPER ROUTE**
70921-X ($3.99 US/$4.99 Can)

☐ **RAMONA AND HER MOTHER**
70952-X ($3.99 US/$4.99 Can)

☐ **OTIS SPOFFORD**
70919-8 ($3.99 US/$4.99 Can)

☐ **THE MOUSE AND THE
MOTORCYCLE**
70924-4 ($3.99 US/$4.99 Can)

☐ **SOCKS**
70926-0 ($3.99 US/$4.99 Can)

☐ **EMILY'S RUNAWAY
IMAGINATION**
70923-6 ($3.99 US/$4.99 Can)

☐ **MUGGIE MAGGIE**
71087-0 ($3.99 US/$4.99 Can)

☐ **RAMONA THE PEST**
70954-6 ($3.99 US/$4.99 Can)

Look for More Mystery Adventure And Fun in the Kitchen With

AND THE CASE OF THE KING'S GHOST
76350-8/$2.99 US/$3.50 Can

AND THE CASE OF THE MISSING CASTLE
76348-6/$2.99 US/$3.50 Can

AND THE CASE OF THE POLKA-DOT SAFECRACKER
76099-1/$2.95 US/$3.50 Can

Each Book Includes Easy-to-Follow Recipes For Cookie's Favorite Dishes!

Coming Soon

AND THE CASE OF THE CROOKED KEY
76896-8/$3.50 US/$4.50 Can

Avon Camelot Presents Fantabulous Fun from Mike Thaler, America's "Riddle King"

CREAM OF CREATURE FROM THE SCHOOL CAFETERIA
89862-4 $2.99 US/$3.50 Can

A HIPPOPOTAMUS ATE THE TEACHER
78048-8 $2.95 US/$3.50 Can

THERE'S A HIPPOPOTAMUS UNDER MY BED
40238-6 $2.95 US/$3.50 Can

Coming Soon

CANNON THE LIBRARIAN
76964-6 $3.50 US/$4.50 Can

WORLDS OF WONDER
FROM
AVON CAMELOT

THE INDIAN IN THE CUPBOARD
Lynne Reid Banks 60012-9/$3.99US/$4.99Can

THE RETURN OF THE INDIAN
Lynne Reid Banks   70284-3/$3.50US only

THE SECRET OF THE INDIAN
Lynne Reid Banks   71040-4/$3.99US only

BEHIND THE ATTIC WALL
Sylvia Cassedy   69843-9/$3.99US/$4.99Can

ALWAYS AND FOREVER FRIENDS
C.S. Adler   70687-3/$3.50US/$4.25Can